Where Is Home, Little Pip?

Karma Wilson illustrated by Jane Chapman

SIMON AND SCHUSTER

London   New York   Sydney

Pip was hatched in a nest made of pebbles on the cold Antarctic shore. She was as fluffy as new-fallen snow and small even for a baby penguin.

Every day Pip played.

Whooosh . . . Whiiiish . . . WHEEEEEE!

Mummy and Daddy always said,
"Don't wander far, Little Pip."

And Pip didn't.

Every night her parents sang . . .

"Our home is where the land is free
From hill or mountain, twig or tree,
In our pebbly nest by the stormy sea,
Where Mummy and Daddy and Pip
makes three."

Pip grew. Mummy and Daddy constantly fished for food for their little one. But they never left her for long and always warned, "Don't wander far, Little Pip." And Pip didn't.

Until . . .

. . . one day Pip saw a feather.

It glittered black against the white ice.

Pip chased after it.

FLAP, FLAP, SLAP

But when she got close a gust of freezing wind fluttered the feather away – POOF!

FLAP, FLAP, SLAP

Pip chased . . .

And chased . . .

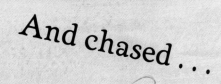

and chased.

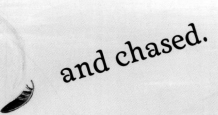

"Got you!"
she cried.

But when Pip turned for home . . .
home wasn't there.

There was no pebbly nest, no penguins,
and, worst of all, no Mummy and Daddy!

"Where is home?" Pip cried.
Nobody answered. So Pip set off to look.

Soon she heard a

SWISH! SWISH!

A mighty blue whale poked her
gigantic head out of the water.

"Hello!" said Pip.
"Can you tell me, where is home?"

The whale smiled. "Yes, little one, I can."

SPLASH!

She slapped her mighty tail and said . . .

"Home is under the oceans deep,
By the coral beds where the minnows sleep,
Where fish are in schools and sea creatures creep,
Where my babies and I swim and leap."

"Thank you," said Pip.
"But that's not *my* home."
And she plodded on.

After a while, Pip saw a
Kelp Gull pecking a shell.

"Hello!" said Pip.
"Can you tell me,
where is home?"

Squawk!

"Yes, little penguin, I think I can."
The gull ruffled her feathers and said . . .

"On the craggy cliffs, in a humble nest,
With sea to the east and land to the west,
In a cosy crevice where shelter is best,
Home is where my little chicks rest."

"But that's not *my* home," Pip said sadly.

"Oh, well," said Pip.
"I'll keep looking."

Pip slumped along.
She had been walking for a long time
when she saw something strange –
a tall, two-legged creature being pulled
by many four-legged creatures.

"Hello, strangers!" Pip called.
"Can you tell me, where is home?"

Woof!

One of the four-legged creatures
wagged her tail and said . . .

"Across the ocean far away,
After sailing a ship for many a day,
On the sandy shore there's a house weathered grey –
Home is where my puppies play!"

"But that's not *my* home," said Pip.

"Nice meeting you. I must keep searching."

And she did.

But the more Pip looked,

the more lost she became.

Finally, Pip stopped. Tears dripped down her cheek and froze solid. Her feet were sore. Her beak was cold. Her eyes were sleepy.

"I want Mummy and Daddy!" she wailed.
"I want *my* home."

Then Pip started to sing . . .

"Our home is where the land is free
From hill or mountain, twig or tree,
In our pebbly nest by the stormy sea,
Where Mummy and Daddy and Pip makes three."

Suddenly she heard something . . .

"Pip? Little Pi-i-iiip? Is that you?"

Suddenly she saw something!

"Mummy! Daddy! Here I am!"
cried Pip.

They rushed to meet her.

They hugged.

They kissed.

Mummy and Daddy danced
and waddled around her.

"Oh, Little Pip!" said Mummy. "Thank goodness we've found you!"
"We heard you singing," said Daddy.
As they all snuggled together, Mummy sighed,
"You must be exhausted, my little one. Let's sleep."

"But aren't we going *home*?" asked Pip.

Mummy and Daddy kissed Pip on her head and they sang a song . . .

"Where is home? Is it far or near?
Is a pebbly nest what we all hold dear?
No, home is where there's nothing to fear.
Since we're together, home is right here!"

And Little Pip slept, safe at home at last.